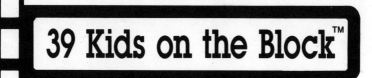

39 Kids on the Block™

The Green Ghost of Appleville

D0110235

39 Kids on the Block™

The Green Ghost of Appleville

by Jean Marzollo

illustrated by Irene Trivas

SCHOLASTIC INC.

New York Toronto London Auckland Sydney

ISBN 0-590-42723-7

12 11 10 9 8 7 6 5 4 3 2 1   9/8 0 1 2 3 4/9

Printed in the U.S.A.   11

First Scholastic printing, October 1989

For Julia

*With special thanks to Nathaniel,
Mike, Leigh, and Lucy*

To Karina

—I.T.

Thirty-nine kids live on Baldwin Street.
They range in age from babies to teenagers.
The main kids in this story are:
Mary Kate Adams,
Joey Adams,
Jane Fox,
Fizz Eddie Fox,
Kimberly Brown,
Michael Finn,
Rusty Morelli,
John Beane,
Maria Lopez,
Lisa Wu

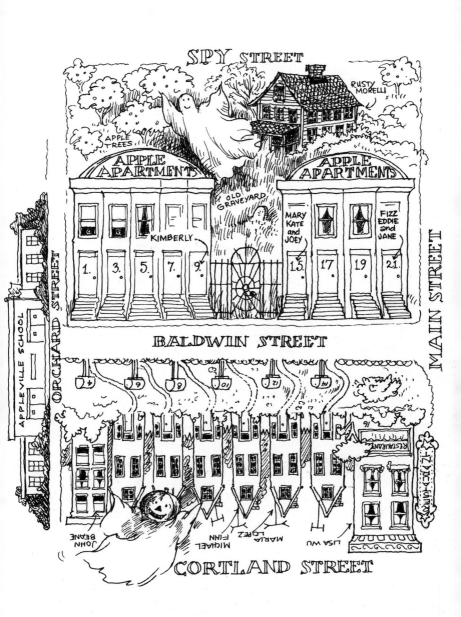

Chapter 1

Mary Kate waited at the front window. She twisted her braids together until they almost choked her. Her street didn't *look* haunted.

But then Mary Kate looked out the side window. Right at the old graveyard.

Kids said the Green Ghost lived there.

Mary Kate's mother said no. There is no such thing as a ghost.

Joey didn't believe her. Joey was Mary Kate's little brother. He was three.

Mary Kate looked at him. Joey was

watching TV. He had his bed quilt around him. It had spacemen on it.

Joey thought the spacemen would protect him from the ghost. So he wore it over his clothes.

Pretty soon Mary Kate's mother would take him, quilt and all, to the day-care center. Then she would go to the hospital. She was a nurse.

Mary Kate looked out the front window again. Down the street came her friend, Jane Fox, with her big brother, Fizz Eddie.

Jane had short, curly blonde hair that bounced when she walked.

Fizz Eddie's brown hair was wet and smooth. He was in junior high school. He got his nickname from being so good at phys ed. Phys ed is the short way to say physical education, also known as gym.

Mary Kate yelled good-bye to her mom and Joey. Then she opened the door and ran down the steps.

Fizz Eddie slapped her five and said, "Hey, man."

Mary Kate and Jane giggled. Fizz Eddie always said "man" to them, even though they were girls.

They loved walking to school with Fizz Eddie Fox. He had a red-and-white jacket with a football on the back. He made them feel grown-up.

It was a cool, crisp October day. Some of the apartments had jack-o'-lanterns in the windows.

"One week to Halloween," said Fizz Eddie.

Fizz Eddie had promised to take Jane and Mary Kate trick-or-treating. They couldn't wait.

Mary Kate was going to be a clown.

Jane was going to be a ballerina.

"What are you going to be?" Mary Kate asked Fizz Eddie.

"Nothing," said Fizz Eddie. "I'm staying home."

Mary Kate and Jane were shocked. "You promised to go with us!" said Mary Kate.

"But then I remembered the Green Ghost," said Fizz Eddie. "So I changed my mind."

"He's kidding," said Jane.

"I am not," said Fizz Eddie. "Last year I saw the ghost. He was light green and had apple-core eyes. He rose up from his gravestone like green slime and looked right at me. Then he went 'BOO!' "

Mary Kate jumped a mile.

"Boo-hoo to you, too," said Jane. "You don't scare me a bit."

"Me, neither," said Mary Kate. But she was lying. And she was afraid. Especially now. They were about to walk past the graveyard.

Every day they walked by it. Most of

the year, they didn't notice the graveyard. After all, there wasn't much to see. Just an old iron fence with a locked gate, one gravestone, and lots of tall grass.

"Look," said Fizz Eddie, stopping at the gate. "See that stone path? It leads to the old farmhouse, right? Last year on Halloween I saw the Green Ghost go up the path, and I saw him go into the *house!*"

Mary Kate got goosebumps.

"What are you scaring those little girls for?" asked Kimberly Brown.

Kimberly Brown lived in the apartment just past the graveyard. She was Fizz Eddie's age. Every day she waited on her stoop for him.

Mary Kate and Jane hated Kimberly because she never talked to them. And once Fizz Eddie met up with her, he didn't talk to them, either.

Now Mary Kate and Jane walked behind

Fizz Eddie and Kimberly. They watched Fizz Eddie's football jiggle and Kimberly's ponytail bounce.

"Do you believe your brother?" asked Mary Kate.

"No," said Jane. "Except for one thing. Last year on Halloween night, he went home early. He said he was sick and went to bed."

Fizz Eddie didn't look sick now. He was laughing and talking with Kimberly. Any ghost that could make him sick must be really awful, thought Mary Kate.

When they got to school, Fizz Eddie tugged Mary Kate's braids lightly. "Be cool," he said. Then he and Kimberly went to the blue door.

The Appleville School was one school with two parts. Each part had its own door.

The kids in elementary school went in the green door on the left.

The kids in junior high used the blue door on the right.

Kirk Malone, the biggest sixth-grader, was the safety patrol leader at the green door. "You walked on the grass," he told Jane.

"I did not," said Jane.

"I won't report you this time," said Kirk, letting the girls pass. "But don't do it again."

"Kirk the jerk," said Jane.

"Jane the pain," said Kirk.

Mary Kate ignored them. She was still thinking about the awful Green Ghost with the rotten apple-core eyes.

Chapter 2

Mary Kate's teacher, Mr. Carson, had short gray hair and glasses. He was wearing tan pants, a yellow shirt, suspenders, and a bow tie.

Mr. Carson's favorite subject was math. He said everything was mathematical.

"What's mathematical about these pictures?" he asked. Mr. Carson pointed to new pictures of witches, pumpkins, and ghosts on the math bulletin board.

Michael Finn's hand whooshed into the

air. He always knew everything first.

"Let's give the other kids a minute to think, Michael," said Mr. Carson.

Jane raised her hand.

"Jane?"

"All the pictures are about Halloween. Halloween is October 31. 31 is a number," said Jane.

"Ooh! Ooh! I've got a great answer," said Michael Finn.

Mr. Carson said to Jane, "You're quite right, Jane. Does anyone else have an idea? How else are these pictures mathematical?"

"Me! Me!" said Michael Finn, waving his hand even harder.

"Michael?"

"Five witches, nine pumpkins, and eight ghosts make twenty-two Halloween things," said Michael. "I added them up."

"Very good, Michael," said Mr. Carson.

"In my head," said Michael. "Without paper."

"Don't be such a show-off," said Mary Kate. She raised her own hand. Gracefully and quietly.

"Mary Kate?"

As soon as Mary Kate heard her name, she yanked her hand down. She had made a big mistake. Now she was going to look worse than Michael Finn. Worse in a different way. A bad way. At least Michael Finn was smart.

"Mary Kate?" said Mr. Carson again.

"I had a question, but it wasn't mathematical. It was dumb," said Mary Kate. She was very embarrassed.

"That's okay," said Mr. Carson. "You can ask it anyway. Many dumb questions are good questions."

Mary Kate spoke quickly. "Is there any such thing as a ghost?"

As soon as she asked the question, Mary Kate closed her eyes. She also blocked her ears so she wouldn't hear everyone laugh.

But no one laughed. Except for one person. Michael Finn.

Mary Kate heard him because she was only pretending to block her ears.

"Excellent question," said Mr. Carson. "Does anyone have an answer?"

Mary Kate peeked around the room. Only Michael Finn's hand was up.

"Are the eight ghosts in the picture real?" asked Mr. Carson.

Maria raised her hand. She was the tiniest girl in the room. She had a very high voice. "Those ghosts are just pictures," she said. "But I saw a movie with a real ghost in it."

"Me, too," said John and Lisa at the same time. Mary Kate opened her eyes all the way.

"Okay, say I put a sheet over my head," said Mr. Carson. "Say you took a movie of me. Would I look like a real ghost in the movie?"

"No," said Jane.

"Yes," said Mary Kate.

"Call on me!" cried Michael Finn. This time he was waving both hands in the air.

"Michael?" asked Mr. Carson.

"The ghost would be a special effect," said Michael Finn. "Like when someone kills someone on TV, and you see blood. It's really ketchup. It's a special effect."

"Right," said Mr. Carson. "Lots of scary things you see on TV are special effects. They are make-believe. Ghosts are make-believe. Make-believe things can be fun. How many of you like ghost stories?"

About half the class raised their hands. Mary Kate was one of them. She didn't want Michael Finn to know she hated ghost stories. She was afraid he might tease her.

"Thirteen people like ghost stories," said Mr. Carson. "See, Mary Kate? Your question brought us back to math."

Mary Kate nodded. She knew the number should only be twelve.

She wondered about the Green Ghost. Who was right: Fizz Eddie or Michael Finn? Was the Green Ghost real? Or only a special effect?

During art, Mr. Carson suggested that the class paint Halloween pictures. "Later on, you can write about them," he said.

Most of the kids painted witches, ghosts, and pumpkins. But not Mary Kate. She painted an apple orchard with ten trees. In the middle she painted a red farmhouse.

"Look at *my* picture," said Michael Finn. "I'm going to be Dracula."

His picture had blood dripping from Dracula's mouth.

"What did you paint that with? Ketchup?" asked Mary Kate.

Michael Finn didn't answer her question. Instead, he said, "What did you paint a farm for? Too scared to paint a ghost?"

Mary Kate didn't answer his question, either.

Chapter 3

After art, the class had social studies, lunch, and recess. After recess came writing.

Most of the kids wrote about their witches, ghosts, and pumpkins. But not Mary Kate. She wrote a letter to Fizz Eddie.

It took her a long time. She had to ask Mr. Carson for lots of spelling words.

"Ask *me* the words," said Michael Finn. "I know how to spell everything. E-v-e-r-y-t-h-i-n-g. Ha-ha!"

Maybe he wanted to be funny and

helpful. But he was getting on Mary Kate's nerves.

She tried not to show it. Instead, she worked on her letter.

When she was finished, Mary Kate read it over.

Dear Fizz Eddie,

My teacher and my mother both say there is no such thing as a ghost.

My mother told me all about it. Where we live was once an apple orchard with a farmhouse. Mr. Green owned it.

Then a developer came. He cut down most of the apple trees. He built the Appleville apartments.

He named the streets after apples. That's why we live on Baldwin Street.

Mr. Green wouldn't sell his house or the old graveyard. Then he died.

No one knows who's buried in the

graveyard. But the house is not haunted.

You must have dreamed up the Green Ghost. Or else it was a special effect.

Your friend,
Mary Kate

P.S. Please take me and Jane trick-or-treating on Halloween. If you do, it will be the best Halloween ever. You'll see.

Mary Kate and Jane walked home from school without Fizz Eddie. He had football practice.

Folded up in Mary Kate's lunchbox were the painting and the letter.

That night Mary Kate heard a cry and woke up. Mary Kate went to her brother. Joey was crying.

"What's the matter?" she asked.

"The Green Ghost," said Joey. "I dreamed he was choking me."

Mary Kate looked over at the other bed. She put her arms around Joey, but he didn't stop crying.

"In school we are studying ghosts," she said. "Ghosts are not real. I'll prove it to you. Wait."

Mary Kate went to the kitchen. She got her painting and letter. Then she went back to the bedroom.

Mary Kate lay down next to Joey. She gave him the painting to look at. Then she read the letter aloud. She changed the name Fizz Eddie to Joey. And she left off the P.S.

Joey stopped crying. He held the painting to his chest and fell asleep.

But Mary Kate was spooked. She had made Joey feel better. But he had made her feel worse.

After all, Joey was just a little kid. He believed whatever you told him.

Mary Kate didn't know what to believe.

She looked out the back window. What she saw made her heart go *boom*.

A light was on in the haunted house.

Mary Kate ran down the hall to her parents' room. They were sound asleep.

She wanted to wake them up. But they thought only Joey was afraid of ghosts. Would they think she was being silly?

Mary Kate glanced out of the window in their room. There was no light in the haunted house.

Had she dreamed it?

Mary Kate went back to her room. She peeked out of her window. The haunted house was dark.

Her drawing was still in Joey's arms. Mary Kate wanted it back. But she didn't want to wake her brother up.

Very carefully, she lay down next to Joey again. She picked up the edge of his quilt and pulled it over her. Just in case.

Chapter 4

"Last night I saw a light in the haunted house," Mary Kate told her father at breakfast.

"I saw the man in the moon eat a pickle," he said. " 'Bye, sweetie. Have to run." Her father left for work.

"Last night I saw a light in the haunted house," Mary Kate told her mother.

"Sh-h-h," said her mother. "Or you'll scare Joey."

Mary Kate waited at the front window. Jane and Fizz Eddie were coming down the walk. Mary Kate ran out to meet them.

"What's up, man?" said Fizz Eddie.

"This is for you," said Mary Kate. She gave him the letter and the painting. They were a little ripped.

Fizz Eddie unfolded the painting and whistled. Mary Kate could tell he liked it.

Then he read the letter out loud. "Hm-m-m," he said at the end. "Just one question."

"What is it?" asked Mary Kate.

Fizz Eddie walked to the graveyard and stopped. He looked up the path to the haunted house.

"Someone turned on the light in the haunted house last night," he said.

"I saw that, too!" said Mary Kate.

"Not only did I see it," said Fizz Eddie. "But I crept up to the house and peeked inside. Do you know what I saw?"

"What?" said Mary Kate. She felt chills

going up her back. She looked over at Jane. Jane's eyes were popping.

Fizz Eddie bent down. He looked very scared and sick. "I saw the Green Ghost cooking in the kitchen," he said. "He was stirring a pot on the stove. I saw him put worms, bugs, and apples into it. He was making *Green Ghost soup!*"

Mary Kate and Jane grabbed each other in fright.

"Why are you scaring those little girls?" said Kimberly Brown. "No one was in that nasty old farmhouse last night."

"That's what you think," said Fizz Eddie.

He took Kimberly's arm and walked ahead with her.

Mary Kate and Jane followed. They were too scared to talk.

Mr. Carson asked the children to sit on the

rug for meeting time. "Does anyone have anything to share?" he asked.

Mary Kate raised her hand faster than Michael Finn. "Last night I saw a light in the haunted house," she said. In a way, she felt proud. Now she could prove that there *was* a ghost.

"Did you say *haunted house?*" asked Mr. Carson.

Mary Kate explained. "There's an old farmhouse with a little graveyard on our street. Jane's brother says it's haunted by the Green Ghost. Last night the ghost was cooking soup. I saw the light."

Mr. Carson drew a chart on the board. On one side he wrote *Ghosts*. On the other side he wrote *No ghosts*.

Then he said to the class, "Raise your hand if you think there is no such a thing as a ghost."

Jane and Michael Finn raised their hands.

Mary Kate looked at Jane. Was Jane telling the truth? Or was she just trying to act brave?

Mr. Carson wrote 2 under *No ghosts*.

Then he said to the class, "Raise your hands if you think there really *is* such a thing as a ghost."

Everyone else raised their hands.

Mr. Carson wrote 21 under *Ghosts*.

If twenty-one kids believe in ghosts, that proves they are real, thought Mary Kate.

Just then, the door opened. Dr. Andrews, the principal, came in with a new boy. He had red hair and freckles. Both of his top teeth were missing.

"I'd like you to meet Rusty Morelli," said Dr. Andrews. "He'll be joining this class. His parents are studying trees in Brazil for a year. Rusty and his grandmother just moved to Baldwin Street."

"That's my street!" yelled Michael Finn.

"Mine, too!" said Mary Kate, Jane, John, Lisa, and Maria all at the same time.

"What number do you live at?" asked Jane.

"Eleven," said Rusty.

Jane and Mary Kate gasped.

"What's wrong with that?" asked Rusty.

"That's the old farmhouse," said Michael Finn. "Some people think it's haunted by the Green Ghost."

Rusty's eyes got wet. He looked as if he were going to cry.

"There's no such thing as a haunted house," said Mr. Carson. He put his arm around Rusty.

Mary Kate wanted to make the new boy feel better. So she said, "I saw your light on last night. Were you and your grandmother cooking something?"

"We were unpacking," said Rusty. "We

just moved in. We drove all the way from California."

"That's pretty far," said Mary Kate.

Inside, she was wondering who was right about ghosts: Mr. Carson or Fizz Eddie?

If Fizz Eddie was right, Rusty and his grandmother would have to drive back to California.

Michael Finn raised his hand. "Are you related to old Mr. Green?" he asked.

"He was my grandmother's father," said Rusty.

"Wow," said Michael Finn. "Your great-grandfather was related to the Green Ghost. Maybe now he *is* the Green Ghost!"

Mr. Carson shook his head. "No, Rusty," he said. "Your great-grandfather started the apple orchard that this school is named for. And we're very glad to have you at the Appleville School. Welcome to our class."

Mr. Carson gave Rusty the empty seat in front of Mary Kate.

She stared at the back of the new boy's head. His hair was the color of a pumpkin.

Poor kid. Imagine having a ghost for a great-grandfather. Imagine having to sleep in a haunted house.

Chapter 5

At lunch kids were talking about their Halloween costumes.

"I'm going to wear my ballerina costume," said Jane. "It's from last year's dance recital. It has a purple satin top and a gold net skirt."

"I'm going to be a bunny rabbit," said Maria. "My mother is making me and my sister twin bunny costumes."

"I'm going to be a robot," said Michael Finn. "I'm making my own costume. I'm spraying boxes with silver paint."

The new boy was eating his lunch very quietly. He hadn't said a word.

Mary Kate looked at his lunch. It was packed in shiny red boxes. In the boxes were little round things.

"What's that?" she asked.

"Sushi," said Rusty. "Japanese rice rolls."

Everyone stared at Rusty's lunch.

"What's that black stuff around the outside?" asked Maria.

"Seaweed," said Rusty. "Want to try one?"

"Yuck," said Maria, making a face. "That's weird."

"I'll try one," said Mary Kate, putting out her hand. She didn't really want to eat seaweed. But she felt sorry for Rusty.

Poor kid. He had to eat seaweed. He had to get used to a new school. His parents were in Brazil. He had to put up with everyone's questions. And worst of all, he had to live in a haunted house.

Rusty put a sushi in her palm.

Mary Kate popped it into her mouth. It tasted salty and crunchy. "Cucumber!" she said.

"My grandmother puts a surprise in the middle of each one," said Rusty.

"Really? Like what?" asked Jane.

"Like watercress or shrimp or ginger," said Rusty.

"I don't get it," said Michael Finn. "How come you eat Japanese food if your last name is Morelli? Morelli's an Italian name."

"My parents study trees all over the world," said Rusty. "Once they were in Japan. So now we eat a lot of Japanese food. My grandmother loves it."

"My father's been to Japan," said Mary Kate. "On business."

"How come you didn't go to Brazil with your parents?" asked Jane.

"They're in the jungle," said Rusty. "There's no school there. I could have gone with them, but Grandma needed me to help her move."

"That's nice," said Mary Kate. But she was really thinking that she would have chosen the jungle over a haunted house.

Rusty turned toward Mary Kate.

"You want to come over to my house after school?" he asked. "I have a real Japanese sword. My dad bought it for me when he was in Japan."

Mary Kate swallowed a bite of her sandwich. She didn't know what to say. She wanted to be nice to Rusty. But she didn't want to go inside a haunted house. Especially where there was a real sword!

"Sorry, but I can't," she finally said. "I have to go home and work on my costume."

She looked down at her peanut butter sandwich and felt like a liar.

The next day Mr. Carson gave everybody an orange card with a word on it.

"All of the words have to do with Halloween," he said. "Let's go around the room and read them aloud. If you can't read your word, I'll help you. Maria, let's start with you."

"Goblin," said Maria.

"Vampire," said Michael Finn.

"Skeleton," said Jane.

"Werewolf," said John.

"Ghost," said Mary Kate.

"Ghost," said Rusty. "We have the same word!"

"Then you two are partners," said Mr. Carson. "The rest of you can find your partners the same way. Find the person with the same word you have."

"Partners for what?" asked Mary Kate.

"For deciding what's real and what's make-believe," said Mr. Carson. "After Halloween you and Rusty will make a report. In your report you will tell us if ghosts are real or not."

"How will we know for sure?" asked Rusty.

"Talk to each other," said Mr. Carson. "Ask grown-ups what they think. Observe. 'Observe' means to look very carefully. Observe and think."

Mary Kate couldn't believe her bad luck. She didn't want to observe and think about ghosts with Rusty Morelli. After all, he was living with one.

At recess Rusty stood by the fence all alone. All the other kids were with their partners.

Mary Kate went over to him. He was drawing a ghost in the dirt with a stick. Mary Kate found a stick, too. She knelt down and drew a ghost in the dirt.

"What do you think?" Rusty asked. "Do you think ghosts are real?"

Mary Kate didn't know what to say. If she said yes, he might laugh at her.

So she didn't say a word. Instead, she

drew another ghost. Then she said, "I'm not sure. What about you?"

Rusty said, "I'm not sure, either."

Neither of them noticed Mr. Carson come up.

"Nice drawings," he said. "Maybe you can make some for your report. Tell me something. What do you think is inside a ghost?"

"Slime," said Mary Kate.

"Applesauce," said Rusty.

"What?" said Mary Kate. She was surprised.

Rusty was laughing. "That's what my grandmother says. She says the Green Ghost is filled with applesauce, bapplesauce, capplesauce, dapplesauce . . . ."

"And fapplesauce!" cried Mary Kate.

Rusty had a million orange freckles on his face. With his top teeth gone, he smiled like a jack-o'-lantern.

Mary Kate grinned.

"I think you two will be friends," said Mr. Carson. "And I think you'll make a fine report about ghosts." Mr. Carson walked away.

"Ghosts, boasts, coasts," said Rusty.

"Doasts, foasts, toast!" said Mary Kate.

Then she got serious. "Do you really think ghosts are real?" she asked.

"Yes," said Rusty. "Especially the Green Ghost."

"Why do you say that?"

"Fizz Eddie told me about him," said Rusty.

"You know Fizz Eddie?" asked Mary Kate.

"My grandmother hired him to cut down some bushes," said Rusty. "He and my grandmother thought up a great idea for my costume."

"What is it?" asked Mary Kate.

"Come over after school and I'll show you," said Rusty. "It won't take long."

Mary Kate thought about it. "Did Fizz Eddie go inside your house?"

"Sure," said Rusty.

"And he didn't get sick or anything?"

"Why should he get sick?"

"Never mind. Forget it."

"You never saw a costume like mine," said Rusty.

"Okay," said Mary Kate. "But first I have to go home and ask my mother."

Chapter 6

Mary Kate's mother had just come home from work. She had taken off her nurse's shoes and put her feet up on a chair.

Mary Kate told her all about Rusty.

"He wants me to come over to see his costume," she said. "Can I go?"

Mary Kate was sort of hoping her mother would say no.

"Of course, you can go," said her mother. "Joey and I will come, too. We'd like to meet our new neighbors. Maybe this will help Joey get over his fears."

*　　*　　*

Mary Kate opened the iron gate nervously. Her mother carried Joey in his quilt up the old stone path. Mary Kate followed them.

Rusty and his grandmother were raking leaves in the front yard.

She didn't look like a grandmother. She wore a Mickey Mouse sweatshirt, blue jeans with paint on them, and red high-tops. On her head was a Dodgers baseball cap.

"Pleased to meet you," she said. "I'm Mrs. Morelli. Come on in and see the house."

Joey started to whimper. "No!" he cried. "Ghosts live in there!"

Mary Kate's mother rocked Joey in her arms. "He's afraid of ghosts," she said. "There's a rumor on our street that this house is haunted."

"So Rusty told me," said Rusty's grandmother. "And you know what I've been thinking? That Rusty and I should invite everyone to trick-or-treat here on Halloween."

"We should?" asked Rusty.

"We should," said his grandmother. "What better place to trick-or-treat than a haunted house?"

"What about the Green Ghost?" asked Mary Kate. "Aren't you afraid of him?"

"Why should I be afraid of him? I'm related to him!" said Mrs. Morelli. "Maybe the Green Ghost will sing on Halloween night. You ever hear a ghost sing? It sounds wonderful. La-la-la-la-la-la."

Joey stopped crying.

Mrs. Morelli handed him a big red apple. Joey reached out for it. As he did, his quilt dropped to the ground. Joey didn't seem to care. He took a big bite out of the apple.

Mr. Carson had told them, "Observe and think." Mary Kate observed Joey carefully. He was acting very strange. Maybe he was under a spell. Maybe Rusty's grandmother was a witch. Maybe that la-la-la song was a chant. Maybe the apple was poisoned.

"She's a witch! Don't eat it! It's poison!" cried Mary Kate. She hit the apple out of Joey's hand. Joey started crying again.

"Mary Kate!" said her mother. "What's wrong with you? How could you be so rude?"

Mary Kate burst out crying.

"We'd better go home," said her mother.

"Wait," said Mrs. Morelli. She put her arm around Mary Kate. "Mary Kate, I'm not a witch, and that's not a poison apple. But what good ideas you have! Will you help us plan our haunted house? We could use your imagination."

Mary Kate wiped her eyes with her sleeve.

Mrs. Morelli handed her a handkerchief. It had a picture of Donald Duck on it.

Mary Kate started to smile. As a matter

of fact, she *did* have some good ideas for making a pretend haunted house. She had read them in a party book.

"You're thinking of a good idea right now, aren't you?" said Mrs. Morelli.

Mary Kate nodded. "You soak raisins in warm water in a bowl," she said. "They get plump and soft. Then you blindfold kids. You tell them to put their hands in the bowl. You tell them they are touching mouse brains."

"Perfect!" said Mrs. Morelli. "Why don't we go in and write down our ideas? This will be the best Halloween ever!"

"I don't think you need us," said Mary Kate's mother. "So I'll take Joey home."

Mary Kate hugged her mother and said good-bye. She was glad her mother wasn't mad anymore.

The pretend haunted house sounded like fun. But still Mary Kate was nervous. She didn't want to go in a *real* haunted house.

"Come on," said Rusty. "You'll be safe. Honest."

Mary Kate took a deep breath. Then she ran up the porch steps.

The living room was full of cartons and funny old furniture. There was a couch with bells and beads on it and a wooden mirror with a pig on top. There was also an easel, many paintings, a bucket of long, thin paintbrushes, and a big black bear rug. Over the fireplace hung a big sword in a black leather case.

"I know just what you're thinking," said Mrs. Morelli. "We could hang up the bear rug under the sword. So people see them when they come in."

Mary Kate laughed.

She looked at the paintbrushes. "Are you a painter?" she asked.

"Painter, bainter, cainter, dainter," said Mrs. Morelli. "I guess so. I mean I *hope* so."

"Maybe you could paint a picture of the Green Ghost and the sword for the haunted house," said Mary Kate.

"Maybe *you* could," said Mrs. Morelli. "But first let's make that list."

Mary Kate, Rusty, and Mrs. Morelli sat at an old wooden table in the kitchen. A white cat jumped into Mary Kate's lap.

"That's Blackie," said Rusty. "My grandmother named him Blackie for a joke."

Mary Kate laughed. "Blackie gives me an idea," said Mary Kate. "Let's make a tape of scary animal sounds. We can play it all night long!"

"Yeah!" said Rusty.

Mrs. Morelli wrote down *Scary animal tape.*

"How about a scarecrow with a knife stuck into him? We can squirt ketchup on the knife," said Rusty.

"Yeah!" said Mary Kate.

Mrs. Morelli wrote down *Scarecrow with knife and blood.*

"We can make yarn spiderwebs all over the house," said Mrs. Morelli. "And hide treat bags. Here's how it works. Say you come to trick-or-treat. You come in the house. You find the piece of yarn with your name on it. Then you follow your yarn to the end and get a treat bag!"

"Yeah!" said Rusty.

Mrs. Morelli wrote down *Spiderweb treat bags.*

"And I'll dress up as a witch," she said. "When kids come to the door, I'll go like this. Hee-hee-HEE!"

Mary Kate jumped. Blackie leaped to the floor.

"My brother will cry," said Mary Kate.

"I won't scare little kids," said Mrs. Morelli. "And if bigger kids get scared, I'll take off my mask."

"Okay," said Mary Kate.

Mrs. Morelli wrote down *Witch costume.*

"Let's build a monster's coffin!" said Mary Kate.

"And let's say the dining room is haunted!" said Rusty. "By a monster who was all chopped up!"

"We can make monster brains from cold spaghetti and oil," said Kate.

"And eyes out of peeled grapes," said Mrs. Morelli.

"And the monster's heart from a cow's heart."

Mrs. Morelli wrote down *Monster body parts.*

When Mary Kate got home, she was very excited.

"How was Rusty's costume?" asked her mother.

"I never saw it," said Mary Kate.

"Why not?" asked her mother.

"We were too busy," said Mary Kate. She told her mother all about the pretend haunted house.

Chapter 7

The next morning there was a big sign on the graveyard gate. It had a painting of the Green Ghost on it. The ghost had a samurai sword.

Mary Kate couldn't believe she had painted it. It looked so good.

Fizz Eddie read the sign aloud:

EVERY KID ON THE BLOCK
IS INVITED
TO TRICK-OR-TREAT
AT THE HAUNTED HOUSE
ON HALLOWEEN EVE
4:30 TO 8:00.
IF YOU DARE TO COME,
SIGN UP HERE.

SEE YOU SOON,
THE GREEN GHOST

"That sounds like fun!" said Kimberly. She had come over to see what they were reading. "I'm going to be the first to sign up." Kimberly wrote her name on the sign.

"You guys go if you want," said Fizz Eddie. "But count me out. I don't want to see the Green Ghost."

"There's no such thing," said Mary Kate. "Really." She reached up and signed her name.

So did Jane.

"Come on, Fizz Eddie," said Mary Kate. "The haunted house will be fun. What are you afraid of? You can't be afraid of the new people. You know them."

"I'm not afraid of the people," said Fizz Eddie. "I'm only afraid of the Green Ghost."

"You really think he's real?" asked Mary Kate.

"I know he is," said Fizz Eddie.

The way he said it gave Mary Kate the

shivers. Was it possible that all ghosts were pretend *except for the Green Ghost?*

Should Mary Kate and Rusty put that in their report? Mary Kate didn't want to tell Rusty that idea. It might scare him too much.

Instead she thought about the *pretend* haunted house. News of it had spread fast. Everyone at school was talking about it.

"Do you think all the kids on the block will come?" Jane asked Rusty.

"I think so," he said.

"All except one big chicken, my brother," said Jane. "How could he be such a fraidy cat?"

Because he knows the Green Ghost is real, thought Mary Kate. But she didn't say that. She didn't even want to *think* it. So she said, "How many kids *are* there on the block?"

"I'll make a map for Rusty," said Michael Finn. "I'll show him where everyone lives. He can circle the ones who are coming. And count them up."

The next morning Mary Kate, Jane, and Fizz Eddie stopped at the gate.

Michael Finn's map was hanging under the Green Ghost sign. The title of the map was *39 Kids on the Block. Circle your name if you're brave.*

Mary Kate's name was circled. So were Jane's, John's, Michael's, Lisa's, Maria's, and Kimberly's. Even Joey's name was circled. But not Fizz Eddie's.

Mary Kate wanted to erase her circle. But that would upset Rusty and Mrs. Morelli. It would upset Joey and Mary Kate's mother, too.

Mary Kate looked at Fizz Eddie knowingly. She understood how he felt.

"Don't look at me that way," he said.

"Please take me and Jane trick-or-treating," said Mary Kate. "And come to the haunted house. It's just pretend. You'll see."

"No way, José," said Fizz Eddie.

"I'll take you, girls," said Kimberly. "I'm not afraid of anything."

"You're going trick-or-treating?" asked Jane. "What are you going to be?"

"Junior high school kids don't dress up," said Kimberly.

The way she said it made Mary Kate and Jane feel like babies.

Later at school, Mary Kate said to Rusty, "I have a new idea for the haunted house. Don't let anyone in without a costume. Even teenagers."

"Good idea," said Rusty. "Have you thought any more about our report? I'm getting nervous about it."

"Me, too," said Mary Kate. But she didn't say any more. She didn't want to tell Rusty that there really *was* a Green Ghost.

So she said, "I was wondering. Does

your grandmother believe in ghosts?"

"I don't know," said Rusty. "It's hard to know when she's kidding and when she's serious."

"What about your parents?" asked Mary Kate. "What do they think?" Then she realized that they were far away for a year. "Don't you miss them?"

Mary Kate shut her eyes. That was a dumb question. She didn't know why she'd asked it.

"Yes," said Rusty. "But it's okay. We talk on the phone, and they send me letters. And my grandmother takes good care of me."

"I like her," said Mary Kate.

"Me, too," said Rusty.

That night after Joey was in bed, Mary Kate went to the kitchen. Her mother was at the kitchen table. She was writing numbers in her checkbook.

Mary Kate told her mother about Rusty's parents.

"Brazil is very far away," said her mother.

Mary Kate climbed up onto her lap. Her mother held her like a baby.

"How long is a year?" asked Mary Kate.

Mary Kate's mother sighed. "Halloween, Christmas, Valentine's Day, Easter, last day of school, summer, first day of school, and Halloween again. That's a year."

"Next Halloween Rusty's parents will be here," said Mary Kate.

"Yes," said her mother.

"Would you ever go away and leave me for a year?" asked Mary Kate.

"Not unless I had someone as wonderful as Mrs. Morelli to take care of you," said her mother.

Mary Kate hoped Mrs. Morelli would be able to take care of Rusty if the Green Ghost rose from the graveyard.

Chapter 8

Halloween was finally here.

Kids brought their costumes to school in bags. After lunch, they put them on.

Mary Kate was a clown.

Jane was a ballerina.

John was a tiger.

Lisa was a princess.

Rusty had on a green sweatsuit with a hood. Little pieces of drinking straws were pinned to him with safety pins.

"What are you?" asked Mary Kate. "A drinking fountain?"

"A cactus," said Rusty.

Everybody laughed.

Even Michael Finn. He laughed so hard, his robot suit almost broke.

"I counted all the circled names on the map," he said when he had calmed down. "Only thirty-eight kids signed up to go trick-or-treating at the haunted house. Who's not going?"

He knew who it was, of course. Everyone did.

"My stupid brother," said Jane.

Mary Kate felt her face get red under her white clown makeup.

"Who cares if Fizz Eddie doesn't come?" said Rusty. "Halloween will be fine without him."

Mary Kate hoped he was right.

A whistle blew. The children got in line in the hall.

Another whistle blew. The children marched out of the school.

They marched around the playground. Music played and flashbulbs popped.

One popped in Mary Kate's face. It was her mother in her nurse's uniform.

After the parade the kids went back inside. They had orange cupcakes and apple juice.

Some of the junior high school kids came by to help. Two of them were Kimberly and Fizz Eddie.

"Hey, guys," said Fizz Eddie to Jane and Mary Kate. "You look cool."

"Thanks, but no thanks," said Mary Kate.

"What's the matter with you?" asked Fizz Eddie.

"You promised to take us trick-or-treating tonight," she said. "If we stick together, we'll be okay."

"But you know how I feel about the Green Ghost," said Fizz Eddie.

"Even Joey is going trick-or-treating at

the haunted house," said Mary Kate. "How can he be braver than you?"

"I guess that's just the way the cupcake crumbles," said Fizz Eddie.

After school Mary Kate went home with Rusty. They didn't talk about their report. Just the pretend haunted house. They had a lot of work to do.

Rusty stuck a knife in the scarecrow. Mary Kate poured on the ketchup.

Mrs. Morelli wove 38 pieces of yarn through the rooms. At the beginning of each piece she put a name. Mary Kate felt bad that there was no name card for Fizz Eddie.

She and Rusty filled the treat bags with candy, apples, popcorn, and raisins.

Then they made a coffin out of a refrigerator box. They put it in the living room. They stuck a fake hand under the lid.

Mrs. Morelli painted a creepy sign. It said, "If you want to see what happened to the dead monster, come in." She hung the sign on the dining room door.

On the dining room table Mary Kate put a bowl of cold, oily spaghetti. "The monster's brains," she said.

Mrs. Morelli put a piece of liver in a flat dish. "The monster's heart," she said.

Rusty filled a rubber glove with water. "The monster's other hand," he said.

Getting the haunted house ready was fun. Maybe this *will* be a great Halloween, thought Mary Kate. Maybe the Green Ghost will stay in his grave and not bother anyone.

Chapter 9

It was four o'clock, almost time for the haunted house to start. Mrs. Morelli fixed up Mary Kate's clown makeup. Then she went upstairs to put on her witch costume.

Rusty put on the animal tape. It was mostly Blackie meowing and Rusty making jungle sounds. He and Mary Kate looked over their work. The best part was the haunted room.

"Even though I made it, I'm going to go through it," said Rusty.

"Me, too," said Mary Kate.

"Hee-hee-HEE!" screamed a voice from the top of the stairs.

Mary Kate and Rusty ran over.

Down the stairs came a horrible witch with a green nose. Some of her teeth were black. In one hand was a broomstick. In the other hand was Blackie.

"Grandma!" said Rusty. "Don't make that noise!"

"Someone's at the door!" screamed Mrs. Morelli. "Hee-hee-HEE!"

It was Jane and Kimberly.

Kimberly was dressed as a rock star.

Jane was dressed as a ballerina in a ski jacket.

"A ski jacket?" said Mary Kate.

"My mother made me wear it," said Jane, unhappily. "Can I leave it here?"

"Hee-hee-HEE!" cried the witch. She grabbed the jacket and threw it in the closet.

Jane looked scared.

"It's just my grandmother," said Rusty.

"Come into the haunted house, my little victims," said the witch. "See if you can find your name tag."

Jane and Kimberly stepped into the living room.

Jane found the yarn with her name on it. She rolled it up until she got to her treat bag.

Mary Kate realized she was starving, so she found her treat bag, too. She and Jane ate the candy.

"This is a pretty scary house," whispered Jane.

"Wait until you see the haunted room," said Mary Kate.

"I'm not sure I want to go in it," said Jane.

"Want me to go with you?" asked Mary Kate. "I know what's in there. It's not that bad. I'll hold your hand."

"Okay," said Jane. "But let's ask Kimberly to come, too."

Kimberly said, "Teenagers don't do that sort of thing. You little girls go ahead. I'll wait out here."

Mary Kate really despised her. She grabbed Jane's hand and said, "Come on. Let's go."

"Where's Rusty?" asked Jane.

They looked around. Rusty wasn't there.

"He must be in the kitchen," said Mary Kate. "Come on!"

She pulled Jane toward the coffin. "See," explained Mary Kate. "Before old Mr. Green lived here, there was a big monster. He died in this house. Someone chopped him up."

Jane looked scared. "Is he in the coffin?" she asked.

"You'll see," said Mary Kate, pushing open the door to dining room.

It was dark except for a flashlight. The flashlight shone on a green monster's mask on the wall. It looked horrible.

"Give me your hand," said Mary Kate. "This is the monster's brains."

She put Jane's hand into the oily spaghetti.

"Ooh, ick, yuck!" cried Jane.

Mary Kate lifted her hand and put it on the liver in a flat dish. "This is the monster's heart," she said.

"Oh, no!" cried Jane.

Mary Kate put Jane's hand on the rubber glove. "And now the monster wants to shake your hand."

"That's just a rubber glove," said Jane. "That's not scary."

"Oh, no? Then what about this?" said the mask on the wall. The mask began to hum.

"Mm-m-m-m-m," went the mask. It looked real. It didn't look like a mask.

"Who's that?" whispered Jane.

"I don't know," said Mary Kate. And that was the truth. She really didn't know.

Neither she nor Rusty had put that mask on the wall.

"Mm-m-m-m-m!" The humming was getting louder. Suddenly the mask moved forward. It had a big green body.

Jane started to cry. "Help! Help!"

Mary Kate didn't know what to do. She wanted to run but she couldn't. Her legs were frozen with fear.

Fizz Eddie was right! There really was a Green Ghost. And it was coming closer and closer.

The ghost was going to grab Mary Kate and Jane. Mary Kate couldn't stand it! She looked around quickly for help.

Her eyes landed on the big bowl of spaghetti. Quick as could be, Mary Kate picked it up and threw it at the Green Ghost.

"Hey, man! What are you doing?"

That wasn't a ghost's voice. That was Fizz Eddie's voice.

Someone turned on the light. It was the witch. "Hee-hee-HEE!" she cried.

Fizz Eddie was sitting on the floor. His mask had fallen off. He had spaghetti all over him.

Mary Kate couldn't believe it.

"You lied to me!" she yelled, punching him with her fist. "You tricked me! You said you weren't coming! I hate you." Mary Kate was so mad at Fizz Eddie that she dumped the bowl of raisins on his head.

Rusty ran into the room. He picked up the bowl. He started putting spaghetti into it.

"Hee-hee-HEE!" laughed the witch again. She picked up some spaghetti and threw it in the air. It landed on Fizz Eddie's head.

"Hee-hee yourself," said Fizz Eddie. But then he started laughing, too.

Rusty threw some spaghetti at him.

Pretty soon, everyone was throwing spaghetti and laughing.

Even Kimberly.

Then she helped Fizz Eddie up and took off his green sheet. "You're a terrible ghost," she said.

"Oh yeah?" he said. "I suppose you could do better."

"I sure could," said Kimberly. "Does anybody have a clean sheet?"

And that was how Kimberly changed from a rock star to a ghost in one minute.

She was a good ghost, too. All evening she stayed in the haunted room. She made up great stories about the chopped-up monster. The older the kids, the scarier the stories were.

She told a story to Michael Finn that scared him out of his wits. Though, of course, he wouldn't admit it afterwards. But Mary Kate and Rusty were hiding under the table, and they saw his face.

Kimberly put on the lights for Joey and took off her sheet. She told him a funny monster story. It wasn't scary at all.

As for Fizz Eddie, he put on Kimberly's earrings and black leather jacket. He became a rock star and helped kids bob for apples on the front porch.

When he saw Mary Kate come to bob, he said, "I'll never lie to you again, man."

Mary Kate looked at her friend. His earrings looked funny. She reached out and gave him a hug. He hugged her back.

"This is a cool Halloween," said Fizz Eddie.

"I know," said Mary Kate.

Especially, she thought, because now I'm sure about ghosts.

Chapter 10

Halloween was over. Costumes were put away. But Mary Kate and Rusty still had to give their report on ghosts.

They stood up in front of the class. Mary Kate held up a painting of a ghost. "Just because you see a ghost doesn't mean it's real," she said. "There is no such thing as a real ghost."

Rusty started coughing. He said he had caught a cold Halloween night.

"You may get some water," said Mr. Carson.

Rusty went out to the water fountain.

As he left, he and Mr. Carson winked at each other.

Mary Kate went on with the report. "All ghosts are special effects," she said.

The classroom door opened . . . slowly. In came a white ghost. "How dare you say that?" he said. "Ooo-ooh!" The ghost ran up to Mary Kate.

Mary Kate hid behind the teacher's desk. "A ghost!" she cried. "Help! Help!"

But Michael Finn saw her smile.

"That's Rusty," said Michael Finn.

"I see his shoes," said Maria.

"You're right," said Rusty, taking off his costume. "I just wanted to prove that there really is no such thing as a ghost. And that's the end of our report."

"Very good," said Mr. Carson. "And mathematical, too."

Mr. Carson drew a chart on the board.

On one side he wrote *Ghost*. On the other side he wrote *Rusty*.

"How many of you thought that was a real ghost?" he asked.

No hands were raised.

Mr. Carson wrote a big fat zero under *Ghost*.

"How many knew it was Rusty?"

Twenty-four hands went up. Mr. Carson wrote a *24* under *Rusty*.

Rusty looked embarrassed.

"Don't be embarrassed," said Mr. Carson. "Because of you and Mary Kate, no one believes in ghosts anymore."

"Except for the Green Ghost of Appleville," said Mary Kate. "This year I saw him rise from the grave like green slime. He made me feel sick!"

As she spoke, she had a terrific idea for next year's Halloween costume. Maybe Mrs. Morelli could help her make rotten apple-core eyes.

More adventures from
39 Kids on the Block
Look for #2!

The Best Present Ever

Mary Kate wants a puppy.
But her mom says it's too much work.
Jane wants a fur muff.
But her dad says that killing
animals for their fur is wrong.
Michael Finn wants his baby teeth
to start falling out.
And Rusty wants his parents
to come to the class party.
But they are out of the country!
The holidays are coming soon.
Who will get what they want?
Who will get what they don't want?
Read *The Best Present Ever*
and find out what happens!

About the Illustrator

"Jean Marzollo and I have been the best of friends for more than twenty years, and we have also worked together on many books," says Irene Trivas. "She writes about kids; I draw them.

"Once upon a time, we both lived in New York and learned about living in the city. Then we moved away. I went off to Vermont and had to learn how to live in the country. But the kids we met were the same everywhere: complicated, funny, silly, serious, and more imaginative than any grown-up can ever be."

About the Author

"I like writing about children and their families," says author Jean Marzollo. "Children are never boring. Whenever I get stuck for an idea, I visit a classroom and talk to the kids. They give me millions of ideas, and all I have to do is choose the right one.

"I also like writing about schools and neighborhoods, which are like great big families. People who go to school together and live together learn a lot from each other. They learn to respect each other's differences. Some of my best friends today are people I grew up with and went to school with.

"I remember everything about elementary school—my teachers' names, the lamp with painted roses on it that we gave the teacher when she got married, who cried and why on the playground, and how to make fish with fingerpaint.

"When I write the stories for *39 Kids on the Block*, I draw from my childhood memories and my experiences in schools today. I live with my husband and two teenage sons in Cold Spring, New York, a community with strong values and lots of stories."

Jean Marzollo has written many picture books, easy-to-read books, and novels for children. She has also written books about children for parents and teachers and articles in *Parents Magazine*.

How many kids live on your block?

200 Winners!

Enter the

39 Kids on the Block™

Giveaway!
WIN A BACKPACK!

Wouldn't it be neat to carry all your favorite things in a fun backpack? You can win one! Enter the **"39 Kids on the Block" Giveaway.** Just tell us how many kids live near you on your block, in your neighborhood, or in your apartment building. Then fill in the coupon below, and return by March 31, 1990.

Rules: Entries must be postmarked by March 31, 1990. Winners will be picked at random and notified by mail. No purchase necessary. Valid only in the U.S.A. Void where prohibited. Taxes on prizes are the responsibility of the winners and their families. Employees of Scholastic Inc.; its agencies, affiliates, subsidiaries; and their immediate families not eligible. For a complete list of winners, send a stamped, self-addressed envelope to The 39 Kids on the Block Giveaway, Contest Winners List, at the address provided below.

Fill in the coupon below or write the information on a 3" x 5" piece of paper and mail to: **THE 39 KIDS ON THE BLOCK GIVEAWAY,** Scholastic Inc., P.O. Box 673, Cooper Station, New York, NY 10276.

- -

The *39 Kids on the Block* Giveaway

How many kids live on/in your block? _____ Neighborhood? _____

Apartment building? _____ Other? _____

Name _____ Age _____

Street _____

City _____ State ____ Zip _____

Where did you buy this *39 Kids on the Block* book?
❏ Bookstore ❏ Drug Store ❏ Supermarket
❏ Discount Store ❏ Book Club ❏ Book Fair ❏ Other_____(specify)

KOB489